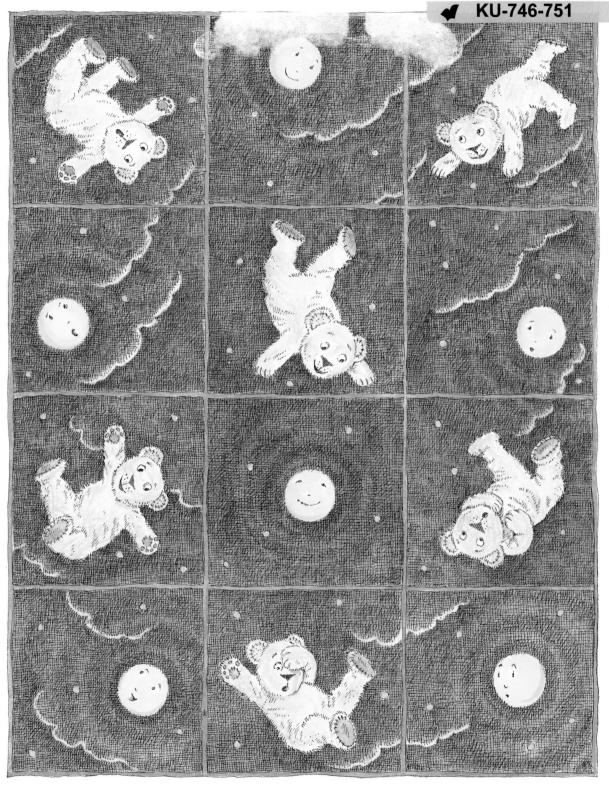

*For Amelia
with our love.*
S.H. & H.C.

First published 1991 by Walker Books Ltd
87 Vauxhall Walk, London SE11 5HJ

4 6 8 10 9 7 5

Text © 1991 Sarah Hayes
Illustrations © 1991 Helen Craig

Printed in Hong Kong

British Library Cataloguing in Publication Data
A catalogue record for this book is available
from the British Library.

ISBN 0-7445-1943-8

THIS IS THE
BEAR
AND THE
SCARY NIGHT

WRITTEN BY
Sarah Hayes

ILLUSTRATED BY
Helen Craig

WALKER BOOKS
AND SUBSIDIARIES
LONDON • BOSTON • SYDNEY

This is the boy
who forgot his bear

and left him behind
in the park on a chair.

This is the bear
who looked at the moon

and hoped the boy
would come back soon.

These are the eyes
which glowed in the dark.

This is the owl
who swooped in the night
and gave the bear
a terrible fright.

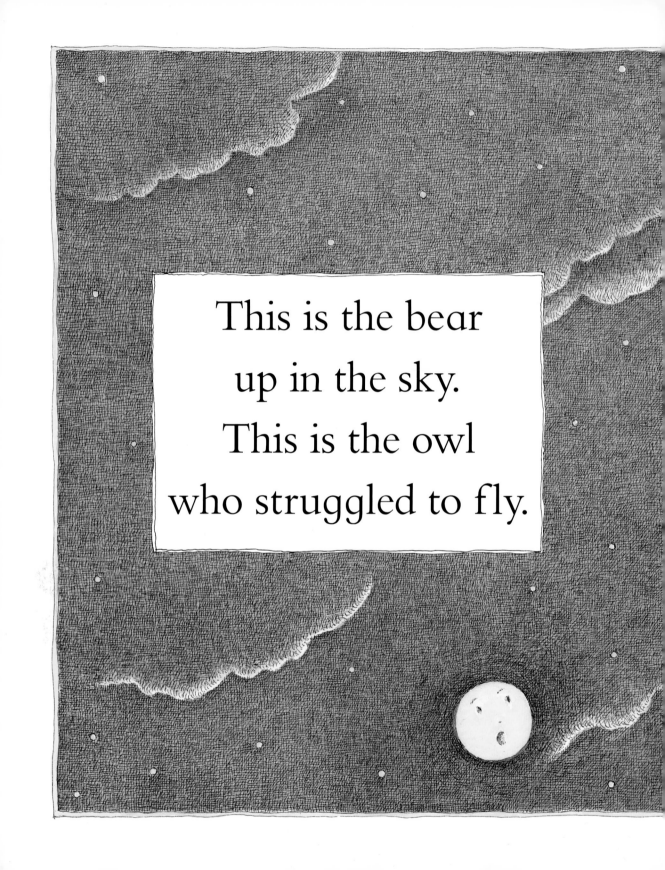

This is the bear
up in the sky.
This is the owl
who struggled to fly.

These are the claws
which couldn't hold on.
And this is the bear
who fell …

This is the bear
who floated all night.

This is the dark
which turned into light.

This is the man
with the slide trombone

who rescued the bear
and took him home.

This is the bear
in a warm blue sweater
who made a friend
and felt much better.

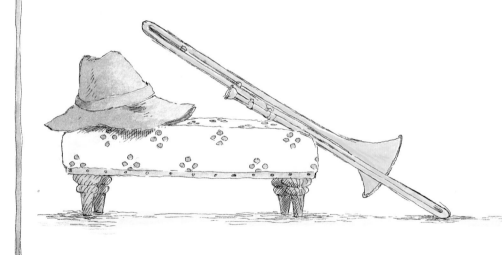

This is the boy
who remembered his bear

and ran to the park
and found him there.

This is the bear
who started to tell

how he flew through the air
and how he fell . . .

and how he floated
and how he was saved
and how he was
terribly terribly brave.
And this is the boy
who grinned and said,
"I know a bear
who is ready for bed."

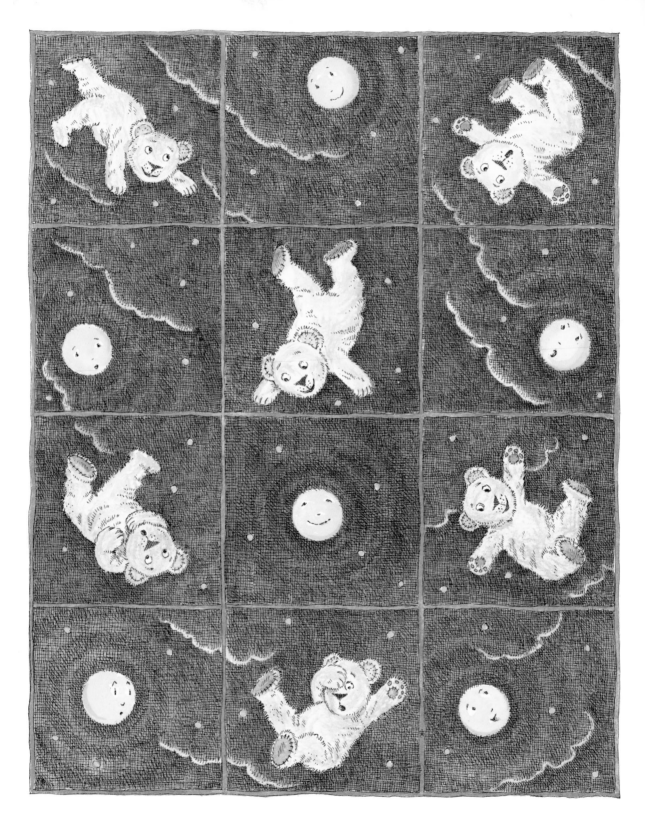